to the Rescue
and other Stories

Scholastic Children's Books,
Scholastic Publications Ltd,
7–9 Pratt Street, London NW1 0AE, UK

Scholastic Inc.,
555 Broadway, New York, NY 10012-3999, USA

Scholastic Canada Ltd,
123 Newkirk Road, Richmond Hill,
Ontario, Canada L4C 3G5

Ashton Scholastic Pty Ltd,
P O Box 579, Gosford, New South Wales,
Australia

Ashton Scholastic Ltd,
Private Bag 92801, Penrose, Auckland,
New Zealand

First published by Scholastic Publications Ltd, 1994
Text copyright © Ruth Silvestre, 1994
Illustrations copyright © Julie Anderson, 1994

ISBN 0 590 55681 9

Typeset by Contour Typesetters, Southall, London
Printed and bound in Great Britain by
Cox & Wyman Ltd., Reading, Berkshire

10 9 8 7 6 5 4 3 2 1

Henry
to the Rescue
and other Stories

Ruth Silvestre

Illustrated by Julie Anderson

For Michael, who reads.

Contents

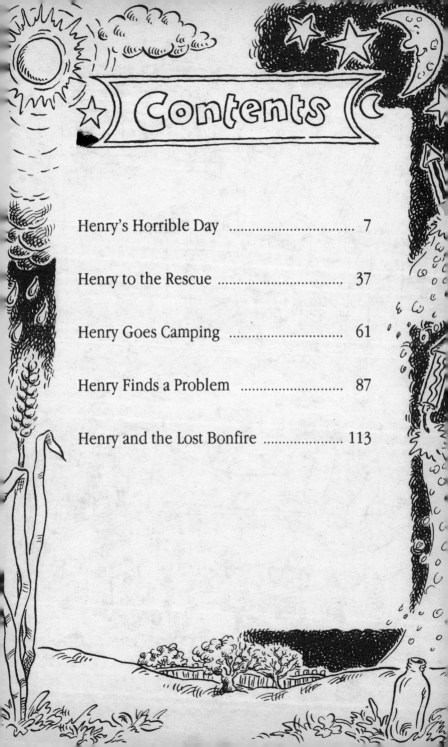

☆ Henry's Horrible Day

Henry got out of bed on the wrong side that morning. Usually there was only one side he could get out because his bed was pushed hard against the wall. But, the night before, he had spent the whole evening playing with his Lego. He had had a great time building a space station. Then he had made three houses for the astronauts to live in and a very long road that went right under the bed and disappeared. So he had pulled his bed out from the wall and built his rocket launcher on the other side.

When he hopped out of his warm bed he was still half asleep and not quite sure whether his mother had called him or not. Too late he remembered why his bed was in such a funny place. "OUCH!" he yelled as his feet crunched down on his Lego.

He was sitting on his bed rubbing his toes when his mother stuck her head round the door.

"Sorry Henry," she called. "I'm afraid I went back to sleep again after your father left and now we're all behind like cows' tails. Do hurry up or you'll be late for school."

"Oh great! Just great!" said Henry. "I'll get a real telling off from Miss, and it's not my fault at all!"

He tugged on his jeans.

"Don't worry, I'll write a note," said his mother. "That's if I can find a pen anywhere in this house."

Henry heard her running down the stairs. "Don't be too long in the bathroom," she called.

Henry dashed into the bathroom and grabbed his flannel. He gave himself what his granny called

'a lick and a promise'. That was her name for the quickest wash in the world.

"Just a quick lick Henry," she would say, "and a promise to do it later."

Henry thundered down the stairs, pushing his arms through his tee-shirt.

"No time for breakfast I'm afraid," said his mother, twisting her hair up into an elastic band.

GOLLY! thought Henry, they must be late. She wasn't even bothering to put any lipstick on. Usually she took ages and put loads of black stuff on her eyes, pulling a funny face while she did it. But not this morning. She must be really late for work too.

"Here, catch," she said, throwing him a banana. "And take that slice of toast. You can eat it in the car."

"Mum! It's stone cold," Henry complained.

"Never mind that. Just think of all the starving children in the world. I'm sure they would just love that piece of toast," said his mother, grabbing her handbag and keys and dashing to the door.

"Well as far as I'm concerned, they're welcome to it," muttered Henry. But he had a nibble as they were driving to school and it wasn't too bad. Not with a bit of banana squashed on it. Better than he'd expected.

The car sped round the last corner and pulled up

at the school gates with a squeal of breaks. Henry tumbled out. Suddenly he remembered.

"The note," he said. "Did you write me a note?"

His mother gave him one of her 'sorry' smiles.

"Oh Henry," she said, "I did find a pen but then there didn't seem to be any paper. I am sorry. Just explain to your teacher – she's sure to under-stand." And she drove off in a rush.

Henry sighed. What a mother! What a start to the day! He looked across the playground and his heart sank. There was no-one there. The bell must have gone ages ago. Everyone was in school. Everyone except Henry. Of course he was late – again. His feet grew incredibly heavy. In slow motion he walked through the school door and down the long corridor to his classroom. On the door was a big 5 and underneath it said MISS BIGGINS.

Miss Biggins was not big. Actually, she was quite small but her voice was ENORMOUS.

"HENRY!" she said, as he tried to slide round the

door without being spotted. Some hope of that! "HENRY!" She said it again even louder. Everyone looked at him. Henry wished with all his heart that he was called Peter or Fred or Leroy or anything at all except Henry.

"Yes Miss Biggins," he muttered. She looked at him.

"And just what time do you call THIS?" she boomed.

Henry looked at the clock on the wall. "Er . . . ten minutes past nine Miss Biggins," he said.

"WRONG!" Miss Biggins was enjoying herself. "Twelve and a half minutes past nine."

Her voice was like an echo in some enormous cave, thought Henry. He would have liked to put his fingers in his ears but he knew that would only make things worse.

"HENRY," she said it again. "You are twelve and a half minutes late. You have wasted those minutes. They will never come back again will they? They are gone for ever." She went on and on and on, but Henry had stopped listening. He knew she would finish sometime.

At last he sat down in his seat. His friend Colin grinned at him. "You've got your tee-shirt on inside-out and back to front," he said. "And you haven't brushed your hair. You look a right mess."

"Thanks for nothing," said Henry. But he grinned back. Colin was all right, even if his mum was always brushing his hair and making sure he was clean and tidy, and always got him to school on time.

"I suppose your mum overslept?" said Colin.

"Right," said Henry. "What have I missed?"

"Not a lot," said Colin. "Have a sweet."

"BE QUIET AT THE BACK!" boomed Miss Biggins.

Henry hoped that the day would improve, but it got worse. He thought he had understood the new sums that Miss Biggins had showed them the day before, but when he took his book up to her desk he found he'd got twenty wrong out of twenty.

"Oh dear, Henry," said Miss Biggins. "I think you and I had better have a little word and then you'll have to do them all again."

Henry groaned.

When playtime came he'd only been out in the playground for five minutes when Fatty Wilson from the top class came roaring round the corner, barged straight into him, and almost knocked him over. Henry felt all the air squeeze out of his body.

He didn't cry but he stood with his hands on his chest and leaned against the wall gasping for breath. Colin put his arm round his shoulders and tried to cheer him up.

"I'm having a really horrible day," said Henry. "I reckon someone's put a spell on me."

"Who?" asked Colin. Colin always asked questions like that.

"I don't know do I?" cried Henry. "But everything's going wrong today. Every single thing."

For the rest of playtime he walked round very carefully and kept out of everyone's way.

After play it was painting and you can guess who knocked over a whole pot of paint. Yes, it was Henry. And guess what colour it was? Black! Actually, Miss Biggins didn't go on too long this time, but she did make him clear it all up. Henry had to scrub the table and the floor and the chair and his knees and then his hands and face as well. By the time he'd done all that, the bell had gone for

dinner and it was too late to paint anything. And Henry really loved painting.

Because of all the clearing up he was the very last one in the dinner queue, and as soon as they got near the dinner hall Henry knew that his bad luck was still following him around. He could smell the smell of his very worst of all dinners – fish. Henry hated school fish. At home his mother grilled his fish or fried it till it was crispy. But school fish was wet and soggy and smelled like old, damp socks.

Henry could only just manage to stuff a bit of it down by hiding each forkful inside a lump of mashed potato.

Perhaps there won't be any fish left by the time I get there, he hoped with all his heart.

The dinner lady put an enormous piece of fish on his plate and then scraped out the last little shred of potato with her long spoon.

Henry was desperate. "Can't I have any more potato?" he pleaded.

"Sorry luv," she said, "that's all there is, I'm afraid."

He watched the dinner lady heave up the great empty pot and carry it over to the sink. "Have an extra bit of custard on your pudding." She smiled at him. Henry looked at her in surprise. What difference would that make? Did she think he could put custard on his fish? People were very odd, thought Henry.

"Swop you some of my custard for a bit of your potato?" he asked Colin.

"I don't really like custard," said Colin.

Henry wondered what else could possibly go wrong on this horrible day of disasters. He soon found out.

Class Five was getting ready for the school concert in five weeks' time. They were learning a funny song with twelve verses and some of the children were going to play instruments. Shirley Brown was to play the guitar, Leroy and Marvin were practising on the steel drums, and six children had been chosen to play recorders. Henry was one of these.

As soon as he heard Miss Biggins say, "Now, where are all my musicians? Get your instruments ready," his heart sank into his trainers. The other five children reached into their desks. They had all remembered, but Henry knew perfectly well where his recorder was. It was at home, lying on his bedside table. In all that dash to get to school he'd completely forgotten it.

"Oh HENRY! Don't tell me you've forgotten your recorder?" called Miss Biggins, right across the room.

The whole class turned to look at him. He didn't need to say anything. He looked so miserable.

"Never mind, Henry," said Miss Biggins. "But I'm afraid you'll just have to sit and listen. It's not your day, is it?"

Henry wondered whose day it was. What made it worse was that Henry enjoyed playing the recorder. He had been practising hard at home, and knew his tune off by heart without even one look at the music. Now he had to listen to the others making lots of mistakes and he ground his teeth with rage. This was the most horrible day of his whole life.

He looked up. There it was on the blackboard. Miss Biggins always wrote up the date first thing every morning. Henry wished he could turn a handle and speed this day up, make it rush by like one of those old black and white films on TV. He would turn it faster and faster until it was all used up: 2 o'clock, 3.30: home and tea. 5 o'clock. 6 o'clock. 7 o'clock: TV, bath and snuggle up in bed. 9 o'clock, 10 o'clock. Sleep, sleep, snore, snore. 11 o'clock, midnight and HOORAY, his horrible day would be over and done with forever. And maybe tomorrow would be his day. But maybe it wouldn't. Henry didn't know what to think at all.

At the end of the afternoon he was carrying a pile of books back to the library shelf. Suddenly they

began to topple, and before Henry could do anything the whole lot fell to the floor.

"OH, DRAT AND BLAST IT ALL!" shouted Henry, and he jumped up and down with fury. Miss Biggins looked at him over her glasses and then said, in a surprisingly quiet voice, "Do you know Henry, I think you must have got out of bed on the wrong side this morning."

Henry was astonished. He looked at her with his mouth open. Perhaps Miss Biggins had magic powers.

"How can you tell that?" he asked.

"It shows on your face," she said.

"I don't understand why," said Henry. "It wasn't my face I hurt, it was my feet."

Now Miss Biggins looked puzzled. "When?" she asked.

"This morning," cried Henry, "when I jumped out of bed on the wrong side."

Miss Biggins laughed. "Hoot, hoot," she went. Henry couldn't see anything to laugh at.

"Do you think that's why I'm having all this terrible luck today?" he asked. "Because I got out of bed on the wrong side this morning?"

Miss Biggins shook her head. "I don't really think so," she said. "That's just something people say when someone is in a really cross mood."

"Why?" asked Henry.

"I don't know," said Miss Biggins. "Come on Henry, let me help you with all these books, or we'll be here all night."

Henry walked home from school very gloomily. What other disasters were about to happen, he wondered? He held his sweet money very tightly in case he dropped it. He was sure it would roll down the nearest drain. He looked up at the sky. Perhaps a thunderstorm would begin and he'd be struck by lightning. He was just thinking that perhaps an alien space-ship would come down and snatch him up to another planet when he reached his own house and went in.

"Hello Henry," said his mother. "How are things? Had a good day?"

"Terrible!" said Henry. "I've just had the worst day of my whole life."

"Poor old you," said his mother. "Do you think you could just pop down to the corner shop and get me some sugar? I completely forgot it."

Henry sighed. "Then I'll make a cake," said his mother, smiling at him with her head on one side.

"All right," said Henry. He was extremely fond of the cakes his mother made when she was in a baking mood. "But I warn you Mum," he went on, "there's a terrible spell on me today. Absolutely everything has gone wrong. It wouldn't surprise me if the sugar bag exploded and all the sugar disappeared."

"Goodness me," said his mother. "Is it as bad as that? Here, you'd better put it in this carrier bag. And do cheer up Henry. Even the worst spell can't last for ever."

"I'll be jolly glad when this one wears out," muttered Henry, as he walked down the road to the shop.

"Hullo Henry," said Mrs Owen who kept the shop. "You look a bit under the weather."

"I'm not under the weather," said Henry, "I'm

just under a sort of bad luck spell. You see I got out of bed on the wrong side this morning. Everything's gone wrong."

"Everybody gets a day like that once in a while," said Mrs Owen. "Your luck will soon change Henry. You'll see."

"I certainly hope so," said Henry, putting the sugar into the carrier bag.

On the way home he passed Mrs Owen's house. Her fat black cat was lying on top of her garden

wall. His name was Percy and he was the friendliest cat ever. He came racing along the wall. Henry stroked him right from his ears to the very tip of his long, strong tail. Purr, purr went Percy. He had the loudest purr you ever heard. It was more like a tiger than a cat.

He began to play a game with Henry. He ran along the top of the side wall to Mrs Owen's garden, and then lay down to have his tummy tickled. He would pretend to bite Henry's hand and then he would uncurl himself and run further down the wall towards Mrs Owen's back door and begin again. Henry pushed open the gate and followed him. He liked Percy. He wished that he could have a cat or a dog of his own, but his mother always said that she had enough to do looking after Henry and his father. She couldn't manage anyone else.

Suddenly Henry stopped playing. He stood completely still. He didn't even breathe. Percy didn't understand and he kept nudging Henry's hand with his hard, damp nose.

"Ssh, not now Percy," whispered Henry. He was listening as hard as he could. He thought he had heard a voice, a man's voice in Mrs Owen's house. Who could it be?

Mrs Owen had just served him in the shop. Henry knew that if the gas man or the decorator needed to get in to her house, Mrs Owen always left her keys with his mother. So what was going on? Henry felt worried.

Silently, he crept nearer to the back door and then he saw that it was half open. He could see the black and white tiles of Mrs Owen's kitchen floor *and* – Henry gasped and his eyes opened very wide – on the kitchen floor, he could see Mrs Owen's clock. What was it doing there?

It was her very special and favourite clock, and Henry knew that it lived on the mantelpiece in the sitting room. It was black with gold numbers on it and on the top of the clock was a bell and two golden angels. When it struck the hour the angels turned slowly and touched the bell. Sometimes Henry took a slice of his mother's cake to Mrs Owen and she would gently move the gold hands of the clock until it struck and Henry could watch the angels turn. Mrs Owen had told him that it had belonged to her grandmother and was worth a lot of money, but she wouldn't part with it. And there it was on the kitchen floor! Someone must have put it there. And what was that next to it? He stared. It was Mrs Owen's radio that she kept by her bed. Henry now knew just what was going on. There were burglars in Mrs Owen's house and they were collecting up all her valuable things to steal them. What could he do? He must stop them somehow.

Henry was scared but he was also very angry. He thought hard. If one of them looks out now and sees me standing here staring he'll know I've seen what they're up to, he said to himself. I must look

as though I haven't noticed anything.

"Come on Percy," he whispered.

He picked up the cat and strolled slowly and softly back down the path. If the burglars looked out now they would think they were safe. But once he reached the pavement, Henry dropped Percy and ran like the wind back home. In the door he dashed.

"Henry, did you get the . . ." his mother began, but Henry didn't stop. Through the kitchen and into the hall he pelted. He knew exactly what he must do. His father had always told him, "In an emergency Henry, you just get to the nearest telephone and you dial 999." And that's what Henry did.

He heard it ring and then, "Which service do you require?" asked a calm voice.

"The police," shouted Henry. "There are some burglars in Mrs Owen's house. Hurry up please."

The police asked him his name and address and Mrs Owen's address too and then said, "Well done Sonny. We'll be along right away."

Henry and his mother watched through the front room window. It wasn't long before a police car raced round the corner and stopped outside. Three policemen jumped out and ran up Mrs Owen's path. Henry and his mother went outside onto the front step.

After a few minutes the policemen came out again with two young men. Henry stared at them. He had never seen real burglars before. They looked very cross and sulky. "Not their day, was it?" said his mother. Henry shook his head.

"Do you think they got out of bed on the wrong side?" he asked his mother.

"Who knows?" she said. "Thank goodness you noticed what was going on. What a sensible chap you are Henry."

Suddenly Henry began to feel very cheerful. It was as though he was warming up all through. His bad luck spell had worn out at last. What a relief! He and his mother watched as the policemen put the burglars in their car and drove away.

"Now for my cake," said Henry's mother. "By the way, what happened to my sugar?"

"Golly!" cried Henry. "I left it by Mrs Owen's gate when I stopped to stroke Percy. I'd better run and get it."

Later on that afternoon a policeman came to Henry's house. He sat in the kitchen and ate a piece of Henry's mother's cake. Henry had to tell him everything he had seen, right from the very beginning. The policeman wrote it all down. Henry had to read it through and write his name at the end. He did his very best joined-up writing.

While he was doing this his father came in from work and they had to tell him the whole story once more.

"You've got a bright, sensible lad here," said the policeman. Henry felt very pleased. The doorbell rang again and this time it was Mrs Owen.

"Henry, you are a hero," she cried. "If it wasn't for you I would never have seen my beautiful clock again. What a bit of luck that you were just going past my house at the right moment with your sharp eyes. And there you were, in the shop, telling me you couldn't do anything right today."

"Well," said Henry, "I couldn't until then. Even

Miss Biggins said it wasn't my day."

"She was wrong," said Mrs Owen, "and when I go to the bank tomorrow I shall bring you a reward."

"WOW!" said Henry. "Thanks Mrs Owen."

That night, Henry lay in the bath looking at his toes. He was quite tired. One way and another it had been a very tiring day. He was glad it had had a good ending. When he was putting on his pyjamas his mother came in and sat on the edge of the bath.

"I'm sorry I made you late this morning Henry," she said. "I'll buy you an alarm clock of your very own at the weekend. Then you can wake me up if I oversleep."

"Thanks," said Henry. He wondered if she would remember. Probably not.

Then he thought about the reward that Mrs Owen was going to give him. He was sure she would remember. She could even remember things from years and years ago. Perhaps the reward would be enough for him to buy his own clock. He rather fancied a clock of his very own. Henry yawned. He was just going to climb into bed when he stopped.

"What on earth are you doing?" asked his mother, looking round the door.

"I'm not taking any chances," puffed Henry, pushing his bed firmly up against the wall. "I'm making quite sure I get out of the right side tomorrow," and he snuggled down and was fast asleep before you could say Jack Robinson.

Henry to the Rescue

It was Friday night and Henry was just falling asleep, when he thought he heard an odd little noise somewhere outside. It was a bit like a baby crying but not exactly the same. Henry wondered what it could be. He was the sort of boy who liked an answer to everything but this night he was just too tired to go on wondering for very long. He had been playing football with Colin all that evening until it was too dark to see the ball and he was worn out. So he fell asleep.

But the next morning, when he was pulling on

his jeans, he heard the sound again. Was it a baby? He wasn't sure. Perhaps someone with a baby had come to stay nearby. He opened his bedroom window and looked down into the gardens but there wasn't a pram in sight. Perhaps there was a

new baby in the flats opposite.

At the end of Henry's garden was a fence, then another garden and then the flats. There were five rows of flats, one on top of each other and, above them all, standing tall against the sky, a long row of chimneys with red chimney pots.

Henry knew most of the people who lived up the first staircase. Colin lived at the bottom with his Mum and Dad and his two sisters. Leroy and his Mum and his Auntie Grace lived on the second floor. They kept rabbits on their balcony. And miserable Mr Widget with the big, droopy moustache, who worked in the garage and never stopped complaining, lived on the third floor.

On the fourth floor lived Mr Timothy and Miss Sarah. They were brother and sister and were very, very old. They had pots of flowers on their balcony that they watered every day and Mr Timothy had a telescope on a stand so that he could look at the stars. They were the politest people that Henry had ever met. They always called each other Mr Timothy and Miss Sarah.

"Miss Sarah's doing too much," Mr Timothy would say to Mrs Owen in the shop. "She's not as young as she used to be."

"Don't you listen to Mr Timothy," Miss Sarah

would reply. "He always makes such a fuss about nothing."

"Good day Mrs Owen," they would both say as they left the shop. "And thank you kindly."

Their flat was the neatest in the block, with lace curtains at each window. The flat above them, at the very top, was empty. Henry's mother said that it was waiting to be done up. Some slates had blown off and the rain had made a mess inside. Henry was just going downstairs to see if there was anything for breakfast, when he heard the odd noise again. It was a very unhappy noise. What could it be? He went back to the window. Then he saw Mr Timothy come out onto his balcony. Each flat had two balconies. The one at the front was wide enough for a table and chairs in fine weather. The other balcony was on the side and just big enough for a dustbin.

Henry saw Mr Timothy looking all round his large balcony as though he had lost something.

Then Miss Sarah came out. She leaned over and looked down at Mr Widget's balcony, which was crammed with old wheels and tyres. She looked very worried. Henry watched as she went indoors and then came out again with a saucer and a spoon. She banged the saucer and called, "Where are you, you naughty girl?" Then Henry heard the sound again and, looking up, at last he knew what it was.

High up on the edge of the balcony of the top flat where nobody lived was a very small, white kitten. Backwards and forwards it ran, crying pitifully. It looked down towards Miss Sarah but seemed too scared to climb down. Henry wondered how it had got up there. Perhaps it had climbed up the rope of the dustbin lift, but he thought that only a monkey would be able to do that.

Each Thursday morning the dustbin men came to the flats. Everyone had to put their dustbin onto a special wooden lift that went up the outside of the

building. Everyone except Colin, of course. His dustbin was on the ground like Henry's. Henry always watched the dustmen emptying the bins in the flats. They came very early. They pulled the wooden lift up to Leroy's balcony and shouted, "BINS! PUT YOUR BINS OUT!" Leroy had to help his mum push their dustbin into the lift and the men would haul on the other rope and down came the full dustbin. They emptied it in a flash and put it back on the lift for Leroy to pull it up. When he had taken his own bin off, Leroy would help to pull the lift up to the next floor where Mr Widget would be grumbling away.

"I don't know why we can't 'ave a proper chute, like in them modern flats," he would moan as he huffed and puffed his dustbin on board the lift.

Miss Sarah and Mr Timothy never complained.

"We won't keep you a minute, dustmen," they would call. And, "Thank you so much," as their empty bin came up. Henry really liked Miss Sarah and Mr Timothy. They always stopped and asked him what he was up to and they listened very carefully to what he told them. He could see that they were very worried so he closed the window and ran downstairs.

"Good morning Henry," said his mother. "I'm just dashing to the cleaners with your dad's jacket. I forgot to do it yesterday. Then I might pop into the market for some salad on the way back. Will you be OK for a bit?" And, without waiting for an answer, she rushed out. Henry drank a glass of milk in two gulps, took his front door key from the hook on the dresser and, putting it in his pocket, he banged the door behind him and ran round to the flats.

First he rang Colin's bell but there was no answer. "All gone shopping, I expect," muttered Henry. Colin's mother always took him with her. Henry plodded on up the stairs. He could hear the radio on in Leroy's flat and Leroy's Auntie Grace singing at the top of her voice. Auntie Grace loved singing. On Sundays she sang in church. Sometimes she even sang to the rabbits. Henry wondered whether rabbits really liked singing. All they did was sit there and twitch their noses.

Henry climbed up the next flight of stairs, past Mr Widget's front door with the notice on it saying: PRIVATE. KEEP OUT. As if anyone would want to go in, thought Henry. At last he reached the fourth floor and he rang the shiny brass bell. Miss Sarah came to the door.

"Oh Henry, it's you," she said. "What can I do for you?"

"Well, nothing exactly," said Henry. "I was just

looking out of my bedroom window and I saw you calling your kitten, and I didn't know you had a kitten, and . . ."

"Oh, Henry," interrupted Miss Sarah, "we've only had her a few days and we've already lost her. I can hear her crying but I don't know where she is. I'm so upset."

"I know where she is," cried Henry, "I've just seen her from my bedroom window. That's why I came."

Miss Sarah beamed at him. "Mr Timothy!" she called over her shoulder. "Young Henry's here and he's seen Kitty."

Mr Timothy came running to the front door.

"Come in Henry, my dear young chap, come in. Come in."

Henry followed them into their sitting room. The walls were covered with pictures and photographs and usually Henry liked to look at them while Mr Timothy told him who they were, but

today they were all too excited about the lost kitten. Henry explained what he had seen and they all rushed out onto the balcony. But although they looked up and leaned backwards, the kitten was hidden from sight because the balcony of Flat 5 where nobody lived was wider than all the other balconies.

"How on earth did she get up there?" cried Miss Sarah.

"I think she must have climbed onto the roof of the dustbin lift on Thursday morning," said Henry. "Then she could have jumped off onto that ledge there. Look!" Henry pointed upwards. Miss Sarah and Mr Timothy craned their necks to see.

"I think you're right, Henry," said Mr Timothy.

"Then she jumped across onto the balcony but now she's too scared to come down," Henry continued.

"Oh, Henry, Oh Mr Timothy," wailed Miss Sarah. "She'll starve to death. She's such a small kitten.

What are we going to do?"

Henry could see tears in Miss Sarah's eyes. He felt very sorry for her. He felt sorry for the kitten too. It couldn't be much fun stuck up on a high, windy balcony with no breakfast, no dinner and no tea.

"Perhaps if we pulled the dustbin lift up again she might climb down," he suggested.

"Brilliant idea!" cried Mr Timothy. "Why didn't I think of that?" They all trooped back through the living room into the kitchen and out onto the small dustbin balcony.

"Now, do be careful," said Miss Sarah as Mr Timothy and Henry began to haul away on the thick rope. It was hard and scratchy and as they pulled, slowly, slowly up came the top of the lift. It was really like a big wooden cage, thought Henry. Except that one side was open to push the dustbin into. There were two thick ropes. One to pull it up and the other to lower it to the ground.

"Heave ho. One more pull," puffed Mr Timothy, and slowly the dustbin lift rumbled into view.

"Right," said Miss Sarah. "Now let's all call her."

"Kitty, Kitty, Kitty!" they cried, looking upwards and watching the ledge. But the kitten did not appear. They could hear her unhappy cry, but she would not jump down.

"Perhaps if we pulled the lift up higher. Right to the top flat," said Henry.

"We can try," said Mr Timothy.

Hand over hand they hauled it up until all they could see was the underneath of the lift with the rope swaying about below it.

"Kitty, Kitty!" they called once more. Miss Sarah banged the saucer with the spoon. Hopefully they waited and then, very gently, they lowered the lift to see if the kitten was in it. Three times they tried. But each time they lowered the lift it was empty.

"It's no use," said Miss Sarah sadly. "I'm afraid she's too frightened and too weak to jump. She's had nothing to eat since Wednesday."

Suddenly Henry had a idea. "If you filled that saucer with food," he said, "I could take it up in the dustbin lift to the top flat. I could reach out and put it on the ledge. She'd smell it and she might even come down to it. Then I could grab her."

"Heavens above!" cried Miss Sarah. "We couldn't allow you to do that. It's much too dangerous." Mr Timothy looked uncertain.

"Well, Miss Sarah," he said, "I'm not sure it's particularly dangerous. But it does require someone extremely sensible and brave, and not too heavy," he added.

"I'm quite sensible. My mother said so. And I'm not too heavy either," cried Henry. "Do let me have a go, Miss Sarah. It might work."

Miss Sarah looked doubtful, but she went to fill the saucer while Mr Timothy and Henry tugged on the ropes to make the dustbin lift exactly level with the floor of the balcony. Then they pulled back the gate so that Henry could step in. Miss Sarah came back with the cat food. Henry didn't think it smelled too wonderful but he supposed it would smell all right to a kitten. Especially a starving one.

Now for it, he thought. Henry squeezed past Miss Sarah's dustbin and stepped onto the wooden floor of the lift. It gave an awful wobble and Henry grabbed the side rail with his free hand. He and Mr

Timothy looked at one another. Henry felt his stomach begin to wobble too and suddenly he didn't feel at all sensible or the least bit brave.

Then he remembered something his father always said to him. "If you're ever in a tight spot, Henry, don't rush. Take a deep breath. And if that doesn't work, take another." Henry took three very deep breaths and felt much better.

"I'm afraid it *will* be a bit wobbly," said Mr Timothy. "But the ropes are fine and you are not nearly as heavy as a dustbin."

"Not a full one," said Henry.

"Now," said Mr Timothy, "you must promise me one thing before we set off." Henry nodded. "You are not, repeat NOT, to get out of the lift. Just remember, boys are more important than kittens. Understood?"

"Understood," said Henry. The wobbles in his stomach had almost gone.

Almost but not quite. They came back again as

Mr Timothy began to haul on the ropes and the dustbin lift began to move. After a few more deep breaths, Henry decided to keep his eyes fixed on the bricks of the wall. Up and up and up he went. Slowly he began to relax. It wasn't so terrible after all. It wasn't as though he was setting off into outer space or going to the moon. Clunk! The lift stopped.

"Are you all right, young Henry?" he heard Mr Timothy call from below.

"Fine," shouted Henry. He could see into the kitchen of the top flat. It looked sad and empty and there were damp patches on the wall. Holding on carefully with one hand, Henry reached up and placed the saucer of cat food up onto the white painted ledge that ran right round the top flat. "Kitty, Kitty, Kitty," he called. He waited and watched. He kept very still.

At long last a little pink nose in a thin white face poked round the edge of the balcony just above him.

"Come on, Kitty," called Henry softly. The kitten stretched her front paws down onto the ledge and mewed. "Come on. You can do it," Henry called again. The kitten looked at him.

Suddenly she made a sort of scramble down with her back legs and wobbled onto the ledge. For one awful moment Henry thought she would fall, but somehow she clung on. She recovered her balance and shot along the ledge to the saucer of food.

"Great!" muttered Henry. "Now for it." In slow motion, as slowly as he could possibly move it, he watched his own hand getting closer to the kitten. As soon as he could touch her he, oh so gently, stroked her skinny white back as she purred and quivered with the joy of eating. Henry waited until the food was almost gone and then he clasped his fingers tightly round the skin at the back of her neck and pulled her down.

"Haul away, Mr Timothy," he yelled. "I've got her!"

Henry hardly noticed the journey back down in the dustbin lift. He held the kitten tight against his chest. Her body was so thin and trembly and her sharp little claws dug into his tee-shirt. Miss Sarah was overjoyed. She took the kitten from him while Mr Timothy helped him down out of the wobbly lift.

Suddenly there was a cheer far below. When Henry looked over the edge of the balcony he saw lots of upturned faces. He saw Leroy with some of his friends, Colin and his mum, (goodness knows what she would say, thought Henry), and HELP! There was his own mother. He suddenly realised that he might be in for a real telling off. And just when he was feeling quite pleased with himself.

But Mr Timothy shouted down, "This calls for a celebration. You must all come up at once."

What a fuss everyone made of him! Mr Timothy opened a bottle of wine and a big box of biscuits left over from Christmas. Henry usually enjoyed a bit of attention but he felt his face going quite red when Miss Sarah cried, "Now, let us all drink a toast to HENRY." And everyone shouted "HOORAY," Mr Timothy played his old fashioned gramophone and Leroy's Auntie Grace sang and they all had a really jolly time. Only the little white kitten didn't join in the fun. She just curled up on a silk cushion and fell fast asleep.

"Well Henry," said his mother, when they got home at last, "I can't take my eyes off you for a moment can I?" But she smiled at him and gave him a hug.

"Do you know," said Henry, "I didn't have any breakfast. I'm starving."

His mother looked at the clock. "It's a bit late for breakfast," she said. "I think we'll have brunch."

"What on earth is brunch?" cried Henry.

"Half breakfast, half lunch," laughed his mother looking in the fridge.

"What a very good idea," said Henry as they began to grill the bacon. "I must say brunch smells a lot better than cat food!"

☆ Henry Goes Camping

"It's raining, it's pouring. The old man is snoring. He went to bed and bumped his head and couldn't get up in the morning," sang Henry at the top of his voice. "It's raining, it's—"

"Henry, if you don't stop that stupid song I shall scream!" said Henry's mother.

Henry and his parents were on holiday, in the country, in a tent. And, as you might have guessed, it was raining.

Henry was on his knees peering out across a very wet, green field. His mother, at the back of the tent,

was rolling up their sleeping bags to look for her wellingtons.

"I know I packed them," she wailed. "How on earth could they have got lost in such a small space?"

"Perhaps they've dissolved," said Henry. "Things do dissolve you know, in acid. Miss Biggins said so. She said—"

"Henry!" shouted his mother. "Do stop talking nonsense."

Henry was about to say that it wasn't nonsense, it was science, but he thought it might be better to wait until the wellingtons turned up. He sighed, and looking out he saw a bigger pair of wellingtons squelching towards him across the grass. It was his father in his shiny yellow raincoat who bent down under the tent flap, his face all red and wet and a trickle of water running off his hair and down his nose. He put his tongue out as far as it would go and licked the drips. Henry laughed.

"Lovely weather for ducks," said his father.

"If you say that once more," shouted Henry's mother poking her head out, "I shall scream!"

"Why don't you just have a good scream anyway?" said Henry's father.

Henry's mother did just that. She screwed up her face, shut her eyes tight, clenched her fists, opened her mouth wide and SCREAMED! She looked so funny that Henry and his father fell about laughing. Henry's mother opened her eyes very wide and looked at them both. Then she grinned.

"Goodness me!" she said. "I do feel better. But I still haven't found my wellingtons."

Henry's father handed her a carrier bag. "Here you are Rosie," he said. "They were still in the car. You forgot to unpack them. Now we can all go for a walk."

"In this rain?" cried his mother, pulling on her wellingtons.

"It's only rain," cried Henry. "We won't dissolve. Oh come on Mum. I've been wet millions of times."

He dashed out, turning his face up to feel the drops. His father zipped the tent up carefully behind them and off they set across the wet, green field.

They had arrived the night before. It was all Henry's father's idea. "We need a change. A long weekend in the country," he had said. He had borrowed the tent from a friend at work and they had practised putting it up in the garden.

Henry was very excited. He had never been camping before. Nor had his mother, but she was not excited. Henry had never seen his father so keen on anything before. He kept telling Henry stories about when he was a boy scout. He went on and on. Henry was surprised, because his father was usually the quiet one of the family, but it was his mother who was quiet this time. She just wandered about with bags of clothes and boxes of food and she kept writing lists and forgetting where she had put them.

"I'm not at all sure this is a good idea," she muttered. Henry couldn't wait to go.

He packed his torch and his penknife and his camera that his granddad had given him for Christmas. He packed a little box of all different sweets and his very own alarm clock that he had bought with his reward money from Mrs Owen.

It had been a lovely warm evening when Henry's father had come home early, and they had loaded the car with all the camping equipment and set off.

"Now, we don't want to stay in one of those big, crowded camp sites," said his father. "What I want you to look out for, Henry, is a nice farm where we can see a bit of country life. So keep your eyes peeled."

"How do you peel your eyes?" asked Henry.

"You just look hard," said his mother. At first Henry tried opening his eyes as wide as they would go but that made him go cross-eyed, so he stopped. But he still looked hard and it was Henry who first spotted the little wooden notice which stuck out of the hedge. CAMPING it said, and EGGS FOR SALE.

"Perfect!" said his father when the farmer showed them his field.

"Where do we wash and where is the lavatory?" asked his mother.

"Oh, Mum," cried Henry. "This is an adventure! You don't have to worry about washing."

"Oh yes you do," said his mother. "Don't forget you're sleeping in a tent with me, and *I* don't intend to keep a peg on my nose for four nights, thank you very much." Henry giggled.

The farmer, whose name was Mr Starling, showed them the 'wash-house' as he called it. It was like a long wooden shed and was very hot inside where the sun had been shining on it. It was quite clean but there were spiders' webs on the ceiling and it was not a bit like Henry's bathroom at home. There was not even a bath – just four wash-basins in a row, two lavatories, and at the end a deep sink for washing up.

"And this tap is your drinking water," said Mr

Starling. "Don't you go drinking out of them other taps."

"Would we be poisoned?" asked Henry.

"I shouldn't think so," smiled the farmer, "but it wouldn't taste too good. Now, would you be wanting some nice fresh eggs?"

Henry and his mother walked across the yard to the farmhouse kitchen. There were rows of muddy boots in the porch and overalls and coats. There were brooms and baskets and boxes and lengths of string. And there were trays and trays of eggs. Henry had never seen eggs like that. They were all different sizes, some brown and some white, and they had bits of feather sticking to them.

"What does that mean, FREE RANGE?" said Henry, reading the notice on the wall.

"It means my hens are free to run about wherever they fancy," said the farmer's wife. "We only shut them up at night to stop the old fox getting them."

Henry wondered if he might see a fox.

It hadn't taken them long to put up their tent and they had set out their chairs and table in the last little bit of sunshine before it went down behind the trees. They had eaten boiled eggs for supper and they were the best eggs that Henry had ever tasted, with the insides bright orange.

"This is the life!" Henry's father had said.

When the rain had started in the middle of the night, it had woken them all up. It made such a loud noise on the roof of the tent. Henry's mother had groaned but his father said, "Don't worry, this tent is perfectly watertight. I tested it. Back to sleep everyone."

Henry had lain very still in his sleeping bag,

listening to the rain. It was very strange. There it was outside, just above, pounding down on top of him, and yet he was all snug and dry. He pretended he was an explorer in the rain forest. Perhaps there were wild beasts prowling around outside but before he could think what sort of wild beasts lived in rain forests, he was fast asleep again.

And now it was morning and it was still raining.

As they all squelched across the farmyard Mrs Starling opened the back door.

"Oh dear," she said. "What a night. You are unlucky. Did you get wet?"

"No," said Henry. "Our tent is perfectly water tight. We tested it." His father smiled.

"Well, according to the radio it's not going to last long," said Mrs Starling. "And I must say, it was just what we needed for the wheat."

"Bread is made from wheat," said Henry. "Miss Biggins said so."

"Quite right," said Mrs Starling. "But have you ever seen it growing?" Henry shook his head. "If you go up the lane past the little wood," she said, "turn right and climb the stile. Then you can walk the footpath to the village and see our wheat fields on either side. In another few weeks we'll be harvesting, so after this lovely drop of rain it's sunshine we need."

"What for?" asked Henry.

"To ripen it," she answered.

"Fruit has to be ripe," said Henry, "otherwise it gives you tummy ache."

"I suppose Miss Biggins told you that?" said Henry's mother.

"No," said Henry. "It was Colin's mum."

Up the lane they walked. The road was black and wet and the hedges full of spiders' webs sparkled like diamonds. Henry sniffed. It smelled good.

"Look," said his father. "There's a weather window."

Henry looked up and saw a patch of bright blue between the clouds.

"If there's enough blue to make a sailor a pair of trousers it will clear up," said his mother. "That's what *my* mother used to say."

The patch of blue was getting wider every minute.

"I should think that's enough to make a sailor a jacket as well and a tent and a sleeping bag," cried Henry. "Hooray. It's going to be sunny again."

Even before they got to the wheat field, the clouds had almost disappeared. They had to take off their coats and the sun made everything steam. Henry thought the wheat looked like giant grass. It came right up to his chest and seemed to stretch for miles and miles. Henry's father picked him a few grains to chew. They tasted sweet and nutty but not much like bread. His father explained how the

wheat had to be ground up to make flour and then his mother told him about making bread, and by the time he had listened to all that they had reached the village shop.

Henry's father was just buying a newspaper when the baker's van arrived with a wonderful smell of newly baked bread. They bought two loaves and took them back to the tent for breakfast. While Henry's father was boiling the water for tea and his mother was trying to remember which box she had packed the bacon in, Henry decided to explore the whole field.

The bit where they had put up the tent was flat. That was very important, his father had explained, otherwise you began to roll downhill in your sleep. But the rest of the field sloped, and as Henry skidded down through the long grass in his boots, he thought he could hear water running. He was right.

"Mum! Dad!" he shouted. "There's a stream here! Come and look!"

"Later on," answered his father, unfolding his paper. Henry found a place where someone had put a branch across the stream and made the water flow through a very narrow gap. Once it had pushed its way through, it ran faster over some stones, and that was what made the noise. He lay on his stomach and looked into the water. It was very clear.

He concentrated very hard. It was a bit like the game they played sometimes in school with Miss Biggins. She would put loads of tiny things on a tray and give them two minutes to concentrate. Then she covered it up and they had to see how sharp their eyes were and how many things they could remember.

Henry noticed the different colours of the stones, the way the plants waved in the water. He saw tiny fish swim out from under the bank and dart back again and suddenly an insect with a brilliant blue body and silver wings hovered just in front of his eyes. Henry thought it was the most beautiful creature he had ever seen.

"Come on Henry, breakfast!" shouted his father.

Henry looked at his watch. It was half past eleven.

"More like brunch again," he cried, as he raced up the field. Goodness he was hungry, and the smell of the bacon made his tummy leap about.

His mother had set the table and chairs out by the fence. She had even picked some flowers and put them in a cup. They had mugs of tea and a plate of bacon sandwiches, and they all sat down with their backs towards the fence, looking down the field and admiring the view.

"This is the life!" said his father. Henry had taken a bite of his sandwich and was holding it in his hand while with his other hand he pointed to a big bird that flew across.

"Look Dad, what's that?" he cried, when suddenly he felt his sandwich disappear. One minute he had it, the next it was gone. He looked at his empty hand. "Where's my sandwich?" he cried.

"You must have eaten it," said his mother.

"I didn't," said Henry. "I only had one bite. I was just holding it like this."

He looked behind him. There was nothing there, only the fence and a few bushes.

"Don't make a fuss, Henry," said his father,

putting down his newspaper and picking up the plate of sandwiches. "Have another one." He handed them across and at that moment a pair of ears appeared over the top of the bushes. A big, hairy face with huge yellow-brown teeth seemed to grin at them and the rest of the sandwiches were pulled off the plate and gobbled up. Henry's mother jumped up and shrieked.

His father cried, "Do calm down Rosie. It's only a donkey, not a dragon!"

Henry just laughed and laughed. He had never seen anything quite so funny. "A donkey! A donkey!" he cried. "Can we make some more sandwiches and can I feed him?"

"I'm not making sandwiches for that brute," shouted his mother.

"Look out!" cried his father, as the donkey stretched out its long neck and gobbled up the flowers.

"Help me move the table," yelled his father, but

it was too late. The donkey snatched his newspaper and began to chew it.

"Look Dad, he doesn't like the taste," laughed Henry as the donkey dropped the paper on the ground. They moved the chairs and table away from the fence and Henry's mother cut more bread.

Mr Starling told them the donkey's name was Alfie. "I should have warned you about him," he said. "I'm sorry I forgot. He's a devil. Eat anything, he will."

"Can you ride him?" asked Henry.

"Best not to try on your own," said the farmer. "He's a bit particular. Might kick out, but we'll see if he takes to you. Bring him a few sugar lumps. He's got a terrible sweet tooth."

Henry went with Mr Starling into Alfie's field. He looked into the donkey's eyes. "Hullo Alfie," said Henry. Alfie put his head on one side then he stretched out his neck and lifted his lips to show his long grass-stained teeth. "I suppose donkeys don't clean their teeth," said Henry.

Mr Starling laughed. "They're not exactly snowy white are they?" he agreed. "Give him the sugar like this. Hold your hand out flat."

Henry looked at Alfie's long teeth. He took a deep breath and held out his hand, two sugar lumps lying on his palm. His hand looked very small and a long way away and Alfie's mouth looked very big. Alfie came nearer. Henry felt the donkey's warm breath. He looked into his glittering eyes as a pair of soft lips snuffled up the sugar

lumps. He heard him scrunch the sugar in his long teeth and then jumped as the donkey leaned forward and nuzzled into his pocket.

Mr Starling laughed and patted Alfie's neck. "Crafty old thing. He's looking to see if you've got any more. But I reckon he likes you. Do you still want a ride?"

"Yes please," said Henry.

Mr Starling made a step with his hands and Henry hauled himself up. Alfie's back was grey and very hairy with a black stripe up the middle.

"Hang onto his mane, there, just between his ears," said Mr Starling. Alfie looked round at Henry as if to say 'not too hard if you don't mind,' and began to trot along by the fence.

"He's jolly bony," yelled Henry.

Henry's father fetched the camera. He took one picture and then ran in front of Alfie to take another. But Alfie decided he'd had enough. He suddenly stopped. He spread out his front legs and

lowered his head and Henry felt himself slipping. Before he knew it, he was lying in the long grass with Alfie looking down at him. Henry was sure the donkey was laughing but he didn't mind. He'd had a ride on a real live donkey and given him sugar. He rolled over and saw that his mother and father were laughing too.

"Are you all right, Henry?" called his mother. "You did look funny. I think I'm going to enjoy this camping after all. You never know what's going to happen next."

Henry and his father grinned at one another. "What did I tell you?" said his father. "This is the life. Come on. Let's all go fishing."

☆ Henry Finds a Problem

Henry was in the supermarket. He was wheeling the trolley while his mother dashed up and down the rows trying to remember what she had written on her shopping list that she had left on the kitchen table.

"Salt?" she called to Henry. "Did I put salt?"

"I don't know, Mum," said Henry.

Sometimes he wrote the list for her while she looked in the cupboard and the fridge. But this time she had met him outside the supermarket after school and, as usual, she was in a hurry. He had tried to tell her what he had found stuck in the bottom of the railings with all the leaves and rubbish, but she wouldn't listen.

It was on the corner of Foley Street, not far from school. Henry, on his way to meet her, was banging a stick along the railings because it made such a great sound. He was poking the stick lower, and watching the bits of paper and leaves fly out when suddenly there it was: another piece of paper but *different*.

Henry just managed to grab it before the wind blew it up the street. He knew it was money, but it wasn't until he unfolded it that he knew how much. Golly! His eyes nearly popped out of his head. It was a fifty-pound note!

"Fifty pounds. Wow!" Henry's heart gave a great leap with excitement. What should he do?

A man was walking along the road towards him. Should he tell him what he had found? Perhaps he was the person who had lost it. But as he got closer he saw that the man looked rough and very dirty and he glared at Henry, so Henry put the fifty-pound note into his pocket and ran off to meet his mother.

She drove into the car park just as he got there. "Go and get a trolley, Henry," she shouted, "while I look for a space."

"Mum," Henry said, when she joined him, looking for her list, "you'll never guess what I've just found."

"I haven't got time for guessing games now," she murmured.

"But Mum, it's—"

"HENRY!" she shouted. "Do you want to drive me completely dotty?"

"No," said Henry. He reckoned his mother was quite dotty enough already.

"Well, let's get on with the shopping then," she said, and she rushed off.

So there he was, in the supermarket, trying not to think about all the things you could buy for fifty pounds. He pushed the trolley faster. He leaned on it with his elbows, taking his feet off the floor. He pretended it was a sledge in Antarctica, gliding smoothly over the ice.

When he got to the ice-cream section he bent forward over the boxes to feel the cool air. He pushed his fingers down into the cabinet. Frost-bite, that's what you could get in Antarctica.

"Raspberry Ripple, Toffee Fudge, Chocolate

Mint," he read the names aloud. He reckoned you could buy the whole lot for fifty pounds. "Mum, can we have some ice-cream?" he called.

"Yes, you choose," she answered.

Henry lifted up the boxes, trying to decide which he preferred. His fingers got colder and colder. This was how you would feel sorting out your supplies in Antarctica, he thought. He wondered whether they took ice-cream. Probably not. He decided on a Neapolitan: chocolate, strawberry and vanilla. He enjoyed mixing the stripes together when the ice-cream was beginning to melt on his plate.

"Henry! Bring the trolley. Do hurry," called his mother. Henry raced round the shelves to where his mother stood. She was trying to balance several packets of biscuits, a bag of crisps and a large box of cornflakes. "What on earth is the use of you coming to help me if you keep dawdling behind with the trolley?" she cried.

"I was just being a sledge gliding in Antarctica," said Henry, "and Mum, I wish you'd listen – I've found —"

"Antarctica! A likely story!" said his mother. "Oh, do come on Henry. Don't just stand there. We haven't got any cheese yet, or butter, or milk." She looked at her watch. "Heavens! Is that the time? We must speed up a bit. I'm going to a meeting. Whizz down the end and get two boxes of orange juice, will you?"

When they got to the check-out, Henry had to help unload the trolley, then put the things into bags and reload the trolley. He raced it across the car park and helped pack everything into the boot of the car and dashed back again to bang the empty trolley into the line. He enjoyed that bit best, and all the time a little voice inside him was saying, "Fifty pounds. Wow! Fifty pounds. Crikey! What could I buy for fifty pounds?" And another much smaller voice inside was saying, "It's not yours Henry. It doesn't belong to you. Someone has lost it."

Henry was very quiet at supper time. So quiet, his father asked him if he was feeling all right.

"Yes," said Henry. "I just don't feel in the mood for talking, that's all."

"OK, old chap," said his father. "You don't have to, but usually we can't stop you!"

Henry didn't feel like talking aloud because of all the talking that was going on in his head.

He lay in bed later and stared at the ceiling. He had a pattern of clouds and stars and a moon. The

moon had a face and when Henry was little he used to talk to it. Now he felt as though the man in the moon was giving him a stern look.

"What are you looking at me like that for?" muttered Henry. "I'm not a thief you know. I didn't steal it. I found it!"

"But it's not yours," said the other little voice inside him. And the man in the moon looked as though he agreed.

Henry turned over and looked at his toys. Fifty

pounds! What could he buy? A racing car set? A radio-controlled hovercraft like Marvin's brother had? Loads of new computer games? Wowee!

But it was the other little voice talking now. Supposing it belonged to a poor old lady and that was all she had? Supposing it was to pay her gas bill and they would cut her off and she would freeze to death? Supposing she didn't have any more money to buy food and she would starve to death? It would all be his fault.

Henry tossed and turned. He should have told his father about it when he came home and then he wouldn't be lying here worrying like this. He heard his parents come to bed. He heard the water running in the bathroom and then the house became quiet. But still Henry could not sleep. He looked at his alarm clock. The numbers glowed in the dark. 23.52 Crikey! It was nearly midnight!

He took the fifty-pound note out from under his pillow and shone his torch on it. It was only a bit of

paper after all – with a silver line through it. *Bank of England* it said, and there was a picture of the Queen wearing her crown. She probably had thousands and thousands of fifty-pound notes. On the other side was a man in old fashioned clothes with very long hair, but Henry couldn't read his name. The writing was too small and he was too tired. He pushed the note under his pillow and, at last, he fell asleep.

His alarm woke him and as soon as he opened his eyes and saw the man in the moon on his ceiling, he remembered. Perhaps it had all been a dream. He rolled over and pushed his hand under his pillow and there it was, a crackly piece of paper. He took it out, folded it up and pushed it deep into the pocket of his jeans. He ate his breakfast and went off to school.

All day he tried to forget about it but he couldn't. It was a bit like having a bomb in his pocket. He felt as though the fifty-pound note was glowing and everyone could see it. And the voice in his head kept on about old ladies starving and freezing. What on earth was he going to do about it? By the end of the day he was really fed up.

"Henry," said Miss Biggins as the class were clearing up to go home, "you still haven't brought me your work to look at. How many times do I have to remind you? Hurry up and I'll do it now before you go."

Henry sighed and by the time he'd found the right book, all the other children had gone. He took it up to Miss Biggins's desk.

"Are you feeling quite well today Henry?" asked Miss Biggins. "You've been awfully quiet and you're very pale."

"I didn't sleep very well," said Henry truthfully.

"Guilty conscience, Henry?" hooted Miss Biggins as though it was a joke.

"What's that?" asked Henry.

"Your conscience?" said Miss Biggins. "It's like a small voice inside you that tells you when you are doing something wrong. It makes you feel guilty. Didn't you know that, Henry?"

Henry stared at her. How did she know? She knew everything, Miss Biggins. She knew when he'd got out of bed on the wrong side. He was sure she must have magic powers. He put his hand in his pocket and pulled out the fifty-pound note.

Miss Biggins's eyes opened wide behind her spectacles. "Goodness me, Henry," she said. "You are rich!"

"No I'm not," said Henry, miserably. Then he told her exactly how he had found the money and how his mother had been in a rush and how he was worried about somebody starving or freezing to death. Miss Biggins put her hand on his shoulder.

"Stop worrying, Henry," she said. "Just take it into the police station on your way home and then you'll feel much better. You know where it is?"

Henry nodded. He felt much better already. He forgot all about what he would buy for himself and he pelted down the street, round the corner and up the steps to the police station.

The policeman sat behind a large desk. He was talking on the phone. "Be with you in a minute, sonny," he said. Henry took the note out of his pocket and laid it on the counter. He looked at it. He was a bit sad about not getting the radio-controlled hovercraft but at least that wretched voice of his conscience had stopped. What a relief!

The policeman put down the phone and came across. He was very tall.

"I found this," said Henry, handing him the note. "In the street."

"I see," said the policeman. "When was this then?" Henry took a deep breath.

"Yesterday," he said very quietly.

"What time?"

"About four o'clock," said Henry. Now the policeman would know that he had intended to keep it. He felt his face going red. The policeman looked him straight in the eye. Then he smiled and said, "Well done lad. Now we must write down all the details."

He got a book from under the counter and showed it to Henry. It had BOOK 89 and PROPERTY FOUND written on the cover.

Henry had to give his name and address and even his telephone number. He began to feel quite important. After the policeman had written it all down he tore a piece out of the book and handed it to Henry.

"That's your receipt," he said. "If no one comes in to say they've lost it within a month, why, you might get to keep it." Henry couldn't imagine anyone not noticing they'd lost fifty pounds.

On the way home he thought about the old lady who would be able to buy her food now or pay her gas bill. Perhaps she might send him a letter to thank him or she might even send him a reward. But the days went by and Henry heard nothing and he was so busy he forgot all about the fifty-pound note.

The whole school had been shown a video about some handicapped children who had to go to a special school called Orchard Lodge. Most of the children were in wheelchairs, and even those who could walk could only go very slowly, using frames or sticks.

"Now, as we are all lucky enough to be fit and healthy," said the headmistress at the end of the film, "we are going to try and raise some money for the children at Orchard Lodge. Would you like to do that?"

The children all shouted "YES!"

"I thought you would." The headmistress smiled. "They want to buy another minibus so that they can all go swimming every week. At the moment they have to take it in turns. She explained that their school was going to organise a sponsored walk. Everyone would get a form with their name on and spaces for the sponsors to write their names and how much they would give for each mile.

Miss Biggins was very keen on the sponsored walk. She even brought a wheel-chair into the classroom and the children took turns seeing how they could manage. It made Henry's arms ache and

he bumped into everything. After only a few minutes he was jolly glad he had good strong legs.

"Where are we going to do the walk?" he asked Miss Biggins.

"In the park," she said. "If we walk right round that is exactly two miles. So we shall try and walk round at least three times."

"I'll do it a hundred times," said Leroy.

"Can we run?" asked Henry, who loved running.

"Of course," said Miss Biggins, "but I think you'll end up walking. Six miles is quite a long way, you know."

"My uncle did the London Marathon," said Marvin. "He could run it a thousand times."

All the children were very excited. Henry got his mother and his father to sponsor him, and Mrs Owen and Mr Timothy and Miss Sarah all promised him 50p a mile. Then he telephoned his granny and she said she would sponsor him too.

"If I do six miles I'll collect eighteen pounds,"

said Henry. "And of course, I might do eight miles or even ten!"

Henry got up early each morning so that he could run to school. He had to get into training. Miss Biggins said she wanted their class to raise the most money. But two days before the great day Henry came home from school with a sore throat, a headache, and the shivers.

"Oh dear, Henry," said his mother. "I think you're in for the 'flu."

"I can't be," cried Henry. "I've got to run on Saturday."

"Well," said his mother, "perhaps you'll shake it off."

"I'm certainly shaking," said Henry, his teeth chattering."

"You'd better get straight into bed now," she said, "and I'll bring you up some supper later."

"I can't go to bed at half past four!" said Henry. "I'll miss all the TV."

But strangely he found that he didn't seem to care what was on television. He just felt rotten and cold and miserable.

The next day he was worse. His head seemed as though it was stuffed with conkers all rattling about and when he staggered to the bathroom his legs wobbled. At the end of the morning the doctor came. Henry lay there looking utterly miserable, the thermometer sticking out of his mouth, while the doctor held his wrist.

"I've got to go running tomorrow," he croaked when the doctor took out the thermometer and held it up to the light.

"No running for you young man," said the Doctor briskly. "Out of the question!"

"But you don't understand—"

It was too late. He could hear him talking to his mother on the stairs. "Keep him warm and still and give him plenty to drink. There's a lot of this around at the moment."

His mother came and put her arm round him. "Never mind," she said. "We'll give you the money anyway."

"But you won't know how much to give," said Henry, "and it's not the same." And he hid his face in the pillow. Even Colin would manage to walk round once, now his mum had decided he could go. And he had so wanted his class to raise the most money and he was letting them all down. Henry thought that he had never been so miserable in his whole life. He fell asleep and didn't wake up until his father came in at midday, and brought him up a glass of orange juice.

"Hullo, old chap," he said. "What's all this about you finding fifty pounds?"

Henry's heart sank. How had his father found out? As if having the 'flu wasn't bad enough! Now he was in more trouble.

"We've just had a call from the police station," said his father. "It seems you're in luck."

Henry's head ached. He didn't understand.

"Nobody claimed the money," said his father. "The police rang to say that they would drop it round." Henry couldn't believe his ears. He pushed himself up on the pillow.

"Wow!" he croaked. "I'd forgotten all about it. I found it in the street, by the railings and, and –" Henry looked at his father.

"And you took it to the police station," said his father. "Well done. Drink up."

There was a ring at the front door and a few minutes later a policeman walked into Henry's bedroom. He put his helmet down on the bed and Henry could hear his two-way radio crackling.

"Hullo Henry," he said. "Well, you did exactly the right thing with this and now it's yours. Sign here." Henry signed his name and his father had to sign as well. "And what are you going to buy with this then?" asked the policeman, handing him the note.

"Well," said Henry, hesitating. "I'm not sure. You see my school are collecting for a minibus and I missed the sponsored walk and . . . but—" He looked at his father anxiously.

"Goodness me, Henry," said his father. "I do think you deserve to keep at least some of the money. You'll still have plenty to take to school. Don't you agree?" he asked the policeman.

"I most certainly do," said the policeman, picking up his helmet. "Well, I must be off.

Goodnight." Henry grinned at his father and suddenly felt much, much better.

His father went downstairs with the policeman and Henry stretched his arms above his head and gave a big sigh of happiness. Miss Biggins would be pleased. His class would be sure to collect the most money, even if he did buy just one present for himself. Now, what should it be? He looked up at the ceiling and for a moment he even thought that the man in the moon was smiling.

Henry and the Lost Bonfire

Remember, remember the fifth of November,
Gunpowder, treason and plot.

This was what Miss Biggins had written on the blackboard that morning when Henry got to school.

"Please Miss Biggins," said Henry, "it's only the twenty-first of October today. I know because it's my dad's birthday tomorrow."

Miss Biggins smiled. "You're quite right Henry," she said. "But I wanted to explain to all the children in the class about November the fifth before it arrives.

"But", said Henry, still puzzled, "November the fifth is Bonfire Night, and we have fireworks. Everyone knows that!"

"Are you quite sure they know?" boomed Miss Biggins. Henry said nothing. It was strange but when Miss Biggins spoke like that he wasn't sure about anything. "And", went on Miss Biggins, "do they all know *why* we have bonfires and fireworks on this special day, the fifth of November?" She looked round the class. "Put up your hands all those who don't know."

Henry stared to see so many hands in the air. Su-Lin who lived over the Chinese take-away, and the new boy who was American and called Jerry, and Helena whose mother was Polish, all put up their hands. So did Colin and also Jamal who came from Bangladesh.

"You see, Henry," said Miss Biggins. "We have to

remember that we have children in our class from all over the world.''

Henry thought that made his class sound very important, but he couldn't understand why Colin didn't know about Bonfire Night. He supposed he must have forgotten. He was always forgetting things unless his mum reminded him.

''Right,'' said Miss Biggins. ''Nearly four hundred years ago—''

''Wow! Four hundred years!'' said Jerry. ''That sure is a long time ago!'' Everyone laughed.

''Yes it is,'' said Miss Biggins, ''and there lived at that time a man called Guy Fawkes.''

''I know, Miss,'' shouted Leroy. ''I know what he did. He made this great big bomb to blow up the King.''

''I don't think they knew how to make bombs four hundred years ago,'' smiled Miss Biggins. ''But you're almost right. You have to remember these three words.'' She pointed to the board.

Gunpowder, treason and plot.

"Gunpowder's easy," said Henry. "It's what they blew things up with in olden times."

"Right," said Miss Biggins. "What about treason?"

"Trees have leaves on Miss," said Colin.

Henry laughed. "Not trees, stupid," he said, "*treason.*"

"Never mind Colin," said Miss Biggins. "You're not stupid. Treason is a difficult word. It means being on the side of the enemy."

"Like a spy?" asked Henry.

"Exactly," said Miss Biggins. "Guy Fawkes was like a spy. And he got together with other spies and plotted to blow up the government. Not a very sensible idea, was it?" she said, looking over her spectacles.

"No!" shouted all the children.

"And I know Miss," said Henry, "in the middle of the night they put all these barrels of gunpowder in the cellars."

"Yeah," shouted Leroy. "But somebody found out and they got caught, didn't they?"

"That's right," said Miss Biggins, "and ever since that day on November the fifth we have bonfires, and we make a guy and dress him up, and collect money for fireworks."

"Wow!" said Jerry, "that's a great story. Wait till I tell my dad. Back home we have fireworks on the fourth of July."

"Perhaps you could tell us about that tomorrow morning," said Miss Biggins, looking at the clock. "You'd better get your shoes and socks off now. It's time to go next door for games."

As they tramped home from school that afternoon through all the fallen leaves on the pavement, they talked about bonfire night.

"Hey," shouted Leroy suddenly, "you know that

big pile of leaves behind the flats that we ride our bikes up and down."

"Of course!" said Henry. "All we have to do is collect a load more leaves and rubbish and we could build a massive bonfire."

"And we could make a Guy Fawkes to put on the top," said Marvin.

"A really good guy," said Henry excited, "so we can collect tons of money and buy hundreds of fireworks."

"My mum says fireworks are dangerous," said Colin.

"Your mum thinks everything is dangerous," laughed Leroy.

"Fireworks *are* dangerous, stupid," said Colin's sister Fiona. "You have to get a grown-up to light them."

"I don't need no grown-up," shouted Leroy, jumping up and down and punching the air.

"Oh, yes you do," said Henry. "And you need a

119

bucket of water and—"

"Yeah, yeah, never mind all that," shouted Leroy. "Let's all go round the block and see if we can find any old furniture and rubbish to put on our bonfire. We'll be the bonfire gang!"

"Great!" yelled Henry. And they all ran down the road, laughing and singing, "Remember Remember the fifth of November."

"Have we got any old furniture, Mum?" asked Henry when he got home.

"It's all old," said his mother. "I've been telling your father for months—"

"No," sighed Henry. "You know – really old, dropping to bits."

"That's what I mean!" said his mother. "Look at this chair. The leg keeps falling off."

"Oh, good," said Henry. "Can I have it for the bonfire then?"

"Certainly not!" cried his mother. "What bonfire?"

"The one in the flats," said Henry. "We're organising it."

"Who's we?" asked his mother.

"Oh, me," said Henry. "And Leroy. And Marvin and his brother and Colin and his sisters and – oh, everyone's helping. We've asked the caretaker. He says it's all right." Henry sighed. "Mum, you *do* know it's nearly bonfire night don't you?"

"Of course I do," said his mother. "But right now I'm more bothered about your dad's birthday. Come and look at the cake I've made."

Henry was surprised as his mother usually forgot, but this time she had made a splendid cake. He helped her stick candles in the big 37 in blue icing that she had drawn.

"How did you remember, Mum?" he asked. She laughed.

"The last time we went to stay with Granny," she said, "I asked her to ring me up and remind me the day before."

"Good old Gran," said Henry. "She never forgets anything."

The next evening Henry stayed in for his dad's birthday tea, but every evening after that he was out collecting rubbish with the bonfire gang until it began to get dark. The caretaker in the flats lent them an old pram.

"Crikey!" said Henry, as they staggered back with another load, "I bet there was never a baby as heavy as this lot."

"I reckon our streets must be the cleanest in the whole town," said Colin's sister. The bonfire grew bigger every day.

They knocked on all the doors and people gave them boxes and cartons, bits of wood, old rugs, old shoes and broken toys.

"Why don't we knock on old Widget's door?" asked Marvin. "He's got loads of rubbish."

They ran up the stairs and rang his bell. They stood outside, giggling and pushing one another. "You ask," they said to each other. "No, you . . ."

Mr Widget looked through his letter box. They saw his cross little eyes and his droopy moustache. "Wot d'you want?" he shouted.

"We're collecting rubbish for the bonfire," called Henry.

"Don't know nothin' about it," said Mr Widget. "Push off." And they all ran back down the stairs again, laughing.

The caretaker, whose name was Charlie, helped

them to keep the bonfire pile neat.

"Mustn't let it get out of hand," he said. "And you'd better get a move on making your guy now, so you can collect for the fireworks. It'll have to be an especially good one because there's a lot about and people get fed up with them."

Leroy's Auntie Grace gave them an old jumper and Mr Timothy turned out an old pair of his pyjama trousers. Miss Sarah showed them how to tie the ends and then stuff them with old newspaper.

"Now I'll just sew him together round the middle like this, with big stitches," she said. "Oh, what fun! I haven't made a guy since I was a girl. Now, how are we going to do the face?"

"I've got this small cushion," said Jennifer, the oldest girl. "I reckon if I push it into the neck of the jumper and then tie it, we can paint a face."

"I've got some paints," cried Fiona. "I'll get them." Soon the guy had a pale green moon face, red cheeks, and round staring eyes. He made them all laugh and Henry got very excited. This guy was beginning to look really great.

"Hands! Hands! That's what he needs now," he shouted. "My mum just threw out some rubber gloves. They'll look smashing. They're in the bin. I'll go and get them." He climbed through the hole in the fence and was back in a flash. He stuffed the fingers with bits of leaves and tied them on with string. Henry waggled the arms up and down and the hands looked really gruesome and wonderful.

"He's going to be the best guy in the world," said Henry.

"I'll ask around and see if anyone's got a really crazy hat," said Jennifer.

"I don't know about 'crazy'," said Miss Sarah, "but I'm sure Mr Timothy has an old bowler hat somewhere. Would that do, do you think?"

"No way, Miss Sarah," said Jennifer. "You can get money for those in the second-hand shop.

Bowlers are really trendy."

"Goodness me," said Miss Sarah. "I'd no idea. I must tell Mr Timothy."

"My Auntie Grace's got loads of hats," said Leroy. "She wears a different one every Sunday. She'll give us one."

"You can't put him in a lady's hat," said Marvin. "He'll look stupid."

"Guys are supposed to look stupid, stupid," shouted Leroy, and they all laughed.

It was beginning to get dark so they sat their guy in the pram and wheeled him down to Charlie's flat. He said he would look after him. "We don't want someone pinching him, do we?" he said. "Not now you've done all this work."

The bonfire gang were really excited. They told Miss Biggins all about it and the class wrote REMEMBER REMEMBER THE FIFTH OF NOVEMBER in big letters, and hung them right across the ceiling. They had meetings after school every day. By the last day of October they had a huge bonfire.

"I reckon we'll leave it at that," said Charlie. "We can't make it too big. They're coming to lop some of the branches off the trees at the back of the flats tomorrow and they've got to have room to bring the lorry in."

"What for?" asked Henry.

"To take away the branches," answered Charlie.

"Why don't they leave them for us to burn?" asked Marvin.

"You don't think they'd do anything as sensible as that, do you?" said Charlie. "It took me a week to get permission for the bonfire. And now all I get is moaning from Mr Widget."

The whole gang groaned.

"Why?" asked Henry.

"Says the smoke will make his flat all dirty," answered Charlie.

"What?" they shouted. They all looked up at Mr Widget's flat. The windows were filthy and the curtains dark grey. It was the dirtiest flat in the block.

"He's a right old misery guts," said Leroy.

"Don't worry about him," said Charlie. "All we have to hope now is that it doesn't rain. Off you go with your guy. Not many nights left, you know."

The bonfire gang's guy was the best in the whole neighbourhood. He had shoes with coloured laces, a red curly wig, a black straw hat with flowers stuck on it and sunglasses. When the gang pushed him out in his pram people stopped and stared. Then they laughed and put money in the tin.

It was two days to go and they had collected nearly thirty pounds. Charlie was to buy the fireworks. He was going into town because it was his day off and they had a better selection there.

After school they all ran round to his flat. Charlie was sitting in his chair looking very serious. He didn't even smile.

"What's the matter, Charlie?" asked Leroy. "Didn't you get the fireworks?"

"It's not that," said Charlie. "I got those all right. It's what went on while I was away."

"What do you mean?" they shouted. "Has someone stolen the guy?"

"No." Charlie shook his head. "I don't know how to tell you!"

"Tell us what?"

"They've taken the bonfire."

There was a shocked silence. Then they all started shouting at once. "WHO? WHY? WHAT FOR?"

Charlie shook his head and held up his hands. "I don't know," he said, "I've only just come home. I went out the back to bring in some of my geraniums and there it was – gone."

They rushed out of Charlie's back door. It was true. There was a great empty space where once there had been their wonderful bonfire.

"But how could anyone just take it?" asked Henry. "They would have needed a lorry."

Charlie slapped the side of his head. "Of course!" he shouted. "That's who it must've been. Those blokes who were sent to clear the branches after the trees were trimmed. I'm getting on the phone right now."

They raced indoors again but there was no one in the office. Charlie said it would have to wait till the morning and they all went home for their suppers feeling utterly miserable.

"Oh, poor Henry," said his mother. "But do cheer up a bit. It's not the end of the world. You've still got the fireworks. Your father has been talking to Colin's dad and Marvin's uncle and they are all looking forward to it."

"But it won't be the same without our bonfire," said Henry. "It was the biggest one you ever saw, Mum. And how are we going to burn our guy, anyway?"

"We could make a small bonfire, I suppose, before Saturday," said his mother. "Just to burn the guy."

"Pathetic!" said Henry and went up to bed. He looked out of the window across to the flats. The garden was dark and misty and very tidy. He couldn't bear to look any more. He was so disappointed. All the next day the bonfire gang were sunk in gloom. They told Miss Biggins about their stolen bonfire.

"Oh, what a pity," she said, but even with her magic powers she didn't seem to be able to do anything about it.

When they got home they all went round to Charlie's. "It was them," he said. "I asked them couldn't they see the difference between a load of branches and a bonfire, but all they said was they were told to collect up the rubbish and that's what they did. We'll just have to make do with the fireworks, won't we?"

At that moment there was a squeal of brakes outside and the slamming of a car door and

Marvin's uncle came in. "I thought I'd find you here," he said. "I'm really sorry about the bonfire but I came to tell you that the Council's giving a great firework display the other side of town, hundreds of pounds' worth of fireworks and a massive bonfire. Why don't we all go? You can take your guy and maybe they'll let you burn him." Suddenly they all cheered up.

"Hundreds of pounds' worth, eh?" said Charlie. "That'd be worth seeing. Ours won't last very long. You don't get that many fireworks for twenty-nine pounds."

And so, on the fifth of November, after they had had their own fireworks, the bonfire gang and all their families and friends went to the great firework display. The bonfire was so enormous it took their breath away.

"Look at that!" said Charlie. "We could never have had one that big." He spoke to the man in charge, and although they already had a guy, they thought that the one the bonfire gang had made was so good they made room for him on top as well.

Once it was alight it burned brightly. Everyone gave a great cheer as orange flames lit up the night sky. There were hundreds of mums and dads and children there and people selling popcorn, toffee apples and fizzy drinks and luminous neckbands that glowed all green and ghostly.

Although they had to stand behind a barrier, they could feel the heat on their faces and smell the bonfire. Everything was very clear in the yellow light of the great fire. Smoke and sparks drifted high in the air and Henry felt very happy. This was even better than theirs would have been.

He stared at the bonfire. It was as big as a house. On one side there were loads of branches and as the flames started to lick up them, Henry saw, high up, a broken doll's chair with a doll sitting in it.

"Hey, Leroy! Charlie!" he shouted. "Look at that! That's just like the one that was on our bonfire. We got it on our first day. Don't you remember?"

Leroy stared. "Yeah, you're right. And look, Mum!" he shouted, pointing. "That's the old roll of black and white lino from our kitchen!"

"It certainly looks like it," said his mother.

"Look, Charlie," yelled Henry, "it's all our bonfire stuff. How did it get here?" Charlie gazed up at the crackling flames and scratched his head.

"You're right," he said. "That lot with the lorry must have brought it here. What a joke."

"We're having our own bonfire after all," yelled Henry. "Hip, hip hooray!"

The bonfire gang cheered and cheered as the first rockets exploded into the sky with showers of brilliant stars in every colour of the rainbow.

BABYSITTERS LITTLE SISTER

Meet Karen Brewer, aged 6. Already known to Babysitters fans as Kristy's little sister, for the very first time she features in a series of her very own.

The Outfit

Robert Swindells

"Faithful, fearless, full of fun,
Winter, summer, rain or sun,
One for five, and five for one –
THE OUTFIT!"

*Meet The Outfit—Jillo, Titch, Mickey and Shaz. Share in
their adventures as they fearlessly investigate any mystery,
and injustice, that comes their way . . .*

Move over, Famous Five, The Outfit are here!·

The Secret of Weeping Wood

In the first story of the series, The Outfit are determined
to discover the truth about the eerie crying, coming
from scary Weeping Wood. Is the wood really haunted?
Are The Outfit brave enough to find out?

We Didn't Mean To, Honest!

The marriage of creepy Kenneth Kilchaffinch to snooty
Prunella could mean that Froglet Pond, and all its
wildlife, will be destroyed. So it's up to The Outfit to
make sure the marriage is off . . . But how?

Kidnap at Denton Farm

Farmer Denton's new wind turbine causes a protest
meeting in Lenton, and The Outfit find themselves in
the thick of it. But a *kidnap* is something they didn't
bargain for, and now they face their toughest
challenge yet . . .